D1631415

THIS BOOK
BELONGS TO

~~Helen~~

Helen

361 00418 4

MADE AND PRINTED IN GREAT BRITAIN BY PURNELL AND SONS, LTD.
PAULTON (SOMERSET) AND LONDON

This book may only be exported for sale in the following territories by the appointed sole agents:
AUSTRALIA—Ponsford, Newman & Benson, Ltd.   NEW ZEALAND—Whitcombe & Tombs, Ltd.
AFRICA—Purnell & Sons (S.A.) (Pty) Ltd.

NODDY GOES TO SEA

BY

Enid Blyton

CONTENTS

1. Noddy's Washing Day
2. Bad Little Tubby Bear!
3. All Very Surprising
4. Out at Sea
5. The Little Mermaid
6. Shell Island
7. It's Lovely to be Home!

LONDON

SAMPSON LOW, MARSTON & CO., LTD.

AND DENNIS DOBSON, LTD.

Copyright © 1959
by Enid Blyton
as to the text herein and
by Sampson Low, Marston & Co., Ltd.
as to the artwork herein

NODDY RUSHED OFF TO THE BIG SHIP, AND THERE
WAS TUBBY STANDING ON THE DECK

1. NODDY'S WASHING DAY

"IT'S Monday morning—washing day!" said Noddy, and he looked out of the window. "Good—it's a fine sunny windy morning—just right for washing!"

He put ready his little washing-tub, and fetched his dirty clothes. Then how busy he was! The lather rose up in the tub almost to Noddy's hot face, and bubbles flew in the air.

> "See me rub,
> See me scrub
> In my little washing-tub,"

sang Noddy, rubbing hard at his dirty little vest.

> "Hear me sing
> While I wring
> Vests and socks and everything!"

7

and there was Noddy wringing out the soap and water, singing at the top of his voice all the time.

"Now you'll go
For a blow,
Flapping in a happy row!"

shouted Noddy, and rushed out to hang them on the line. Mrs. Tubby Bear was hanging her washing out, too, and she laughed at little Noddy as he ran out, carrying his basket of clean washing.

"I never knew such a little fellow for singing about everything," said Mrs. Tubby. "Never! It's really very nice to live next door to you, Noddy."

"Oh—I didn't know you were listening," said Noddy. "Where's Tubby Bear, Mrs. Tubby? Would he like to come out in the car with me and help me to do my shopping?"

"He's in bed," said Mrs. Tubby. "He's been naughty again. Very, very rude to me, and wouldn't even carry out my washing-basket for me! I really don't know what's the matter with him these days. I've sent him to bed for an hour."

"Oh dear," said Noddy, his head nodding very fast. "You should have called out to me—I'd have carried that washing-basket for you! Isn't it a lovely morning, Mrs. Tubby—our washing will soon be nice and dry!"

And away he went indoors, singing loudly again.

"See it blow
In a row,
Flipping-flapping to and fro!"

Mrs. Tubby went into her house smiling. Noddy made himself a cup of cocoa, and then

9

decided he had better go and clean the car. "Washing-day for you too, car," he said, as he went to open his garage door.

He had a look at his washing as he went by. Ah—it was already getting nice and dry! He disappeared into the garage, and was soon busy there.

He heard Mrs. Tubby Bear's front gate click, and saw her going off to do her shopping. Then,

after a minute, he heard something else. What was it?

"It sounds like water splashing about," said Noddy to himself, and he peeped out to see. Good gracious! It was Tubby Bear in the next garden, with the hose—but he wasn't watering the flowers, as his mother had told him to when she fetched him out of his room.

"Goodness—he's watering Mrs. Tubby's nice dry washing and making it all wet again!" said Noddy, in amazement, and he ran to the wall at once. "Tubby! What do you think you're doing? Stop that at once! That's your mother's washing you're watering."

"I know. I'm doing it on purpose," said Tubby. "She was horrid to me this morning. She sent me to bed!"

"Well, stop watering her WASHING!" yelled Noddy.

"Shan't," said Tubby. "Well—yes, I will then —I'll water yours instead!"

And he pointed the hose over the wall and, splishy-splash, the water drenched poor Noddy's nice dry washing. Then he pointed the hose at Noddy and watered *him*!

"You must be mad," said Noddy, feeling the water trickling down his neck. "What's the matter with you lately, Tubby? STOP watering me!"

"I can't," said Tubby, beginning to giggle. "I c-c-can't stop. You look so funny!"

"All right—two can play at that game," said Noddy, very angry, and he ran to get his own hose and turn on the tap. SPLOSH! A great jet of water splashed all over Tubby Bear, and he fell down in surprise.

"AND WHAT IS ALL THIS?" said a loud voice suddenly, and, dear me, it was Mr. Plod, who had come up very quietly indeed. He was MOST astonished to see all this watering going on.

"Oh! Oh, Mr. Plod—it was Noddy who started it all," said Tubby. "He—he was very naughty —he took his hose and wetted all my mother's nice dry washing. Just look at it!"

"Oooh, you bad, un-truthful bear!" shouted Noddy, swinging round, quite forgetting he had his hose in his hand. "Oh, sorry, Mr. Plod! I didn't MEAN to water

MR. PLOD WAS *MOST* ASTONISHED TO SEE ALL THIS
WATERING GOING ON

13

you, really I didn't. Oh my goodness, now *I'm* in trouble too—and all because of that mean, untruthful Tubby Bear. I won't stay here another minute."

And Noddy turned off the tap, leapt into his car and drove top-speed out of the gate, dripping with water. Oh dear, oh dear— what a thing to happen on a nice windy washing-morning!

2. BAD LITTLE TUBBY BEAR!

NODDY needn't have rushed off in such a hurry. Somebody had seen all that happened! It was Miss Fluffy Cat, who had been passing by on the other side of the road. She ran across to poor, wet Mr. Plod and dried him with her hanky.

"Don't blame little Noddy," she said. "It really wasn't his fault! Tubby has been a bad little bear for a long time—and when his mother went out shopping this morning he came out and hosed her nice dry washing—and Noddy tried to stop him."

"Ah—I see—and Tubby watered Noddy's washing too, I suppose," said Mr. Plod, shaking the water off his helmet. "And then watered Noddy, and . . ."

"Yes—and so Noddy got *his* hose, and I don't blame him," said Miss Fluffy Cat, swinging her tail in quite a rage. "That Tubby! He rode his scooter *right* into me yesterday, and never said he was terribly sorry."

"I shall complain to your father tonight, Tubby," said Mr. Plod, sternly. "Just as soon as he gets home."

"Everybody's horrid to me," wailed Tubby. "I shall run away. Yes, I shall! I shall run away to sea! Nobody wants me. Nobody loves me. Boo-hoo-hoo!"

And he ran indoors, not even bothering to turn off the tap. "Waste of good water!" said Mr. Plod crossly, and turned it off himself. "Just you wait till Mr. Tubby Bear comes home! You won't be able to sit down for a week!"

"I'll run away!" yelled Tubby, putting his head

16

out of his bedroom window. "Then you'll all be sorry!"

Well, that night when Noddy got home, tired after a long day's work, taking people to the station and back, and away to the market, and goodness knows what, he heard all that had happened. Mrs. Tubby Bear told him, dabbing her eyes with her hanky.

"Mr. Plod came and complained. And Mr. Tubby Bear spanked Tubby, and Tubby was very rude again and wouldn't say he was sorry. All he said was that he would run away, yes, he'd run away and never come back, because nobody loved him!"

"He won't run away," said Noddy, hugging Mrs. Tubby. "Don't you worry! He'll soon be his nice self again. He's just being silly."

17

But goodness me, in the middle of the night young Tubby Bear *did* run away! Yes—a small figure crept out of the back door and ran quietly down the road with a little bag and disappeared into the dark night. Master Tubby was gone!

Noddy didn't know anything about it till Mr. and Mrs. Tubby Bear came knocking at his door early in the morning. "Come in!" he called.

And in they came, Mrs. Tubby crying, and Mr. Tubby holding a note in his hand.

"Tubby's gone," he said. "Look at this."

Noddy took the note and read it. This is what it said:

NOBODY LOVES ME SO I'VE RUN AWAY TO SEA. TUBBY

"Oh *dear*!" cried Noddy. "Has he really gone?"

"Yes. That's why we've come to you," said Mr. Tubby Bear. "He's taken a little bag of things with him. We think he's gone down to the river, to the jetty there, where steamers and ships tie up. Some of them sail out to sea, you know. Oh, Noddy— *could* you get out your car, and go off to the river, and see if you can stop him?"

"Oh yes—yes, of course I will," said Noddy at once. "I'm almost dressed. I'll get my car. Oh goodness, what a thing to happen! Don't cry, Mrs. Tubby. I'll bring him back, you see if I don't!"

And Noddy got out his car, waved goodbye, and

set off at top speed, hoping that Mr. Plod wouldn't see him go by. He had to stop at the garage and get out of his car for petrol—and who should come trotting up, looking as mad as ever, but the Bumpy-Dog! Noddy didn't see him till Bumpy had leapt lovingly at him and knocked him over.

"Oh, BUMPY! You made me sit in a puddle! Don't lick me like that. Get *off* me, Bumpy. I'm in a hurry, do you hear? Oh, hallo, Tessie Bear! Pull Bumpy off me, will you? I'm in a dreadful hurry. Tubby Bear has  run away to sea, and I'm off to stop him. Bumpy, go AWAY!"

"Oh dear—stop and tell me all about it, Noddy," said Tessie. But Noddy really couldn't stop. He pushed Bumpy away, jumped into his car, and drove off, waving.

20

BUMPY LOVINGLY LEAPT UP AT NODDY AND
KNOCKED HIM OVER INTO A PUDDLE!

"WUFF!" Bumpy ran after the car and leapt in too, his tail thumping against Noddy in delight. He began to lick Noddy's left ear lovingly.

"I've washed that ear already this morning," said Noddy, pushing him away. "Bumpy, get out, please! PLEASE, Bumpy."

But Bumpy sat himself down firmly. He loved Noddy very much, and he wasn't going to miss this ride for anything. What a dog!

Noddy sighed and went on and on, driving fast. WHAT a pity Bumpy had to choose to come with him just now!

3. ALL VERY SURPRISING

NODDY drove on till he came to the river. His car ran on to the big stone jetty, where one steamer and several ships lay, safely tied to mooring posts. Was there any sign of Tubby?

Noddy left his car on the jetty and went to look for him. "Stay in the car," he said to Bumpy. "And look after it for me. You're a nuisance, so do try and make yourself useful for once."

Noddy went to the nearest ship, and hailed a sailor doll on board. "Hey! Have you seen a little brown bear running away?"

"One went on board that big sailing ship at the end there!" said the sailor, pointing. "Better hurry up if you want him—the ship's just casting off."

Noddy rushed off to the big ship. Yes— the ropes were being cast off—and there was

Tubby Bear standing on the deck, looking rather lonely!

"Tubby! Come back!" yelled Noddy, but Tubby shook his head.

"I'll come and get you!" shouted Noddy, and climbed on board the ship. And just at that very moment the last rope was cast off, and the ship floated away from the stone jetty!

"Oh, my car!" said Noddy, in alarm. "Oh, turn back the ship! Look, I've left my car there!"

Bumpy-Dog was most upset to see Noddy jump on board the ship. He leapt out of the car and raced down the jetty—and oh dear, the car ran down too. Bumpy leapt into the water to swim to Noddy and the car fell over the jetty-side, and went into the river with a most tremendous SPLASH!

"My CAR! My car's

fallen in!" yelled Noddy, dancing about in alarm.
"Stop the ship! Pick up my car. It will drown!

Hark at it hooting for
help!"

"Parp-parp!" said the
car, bobbing about on
the water. "PARPARP-
PARPARPARP!"

It was mostly made of
wood so it didn't sink,
but it certainly sounded
very upset. Two sailors ran to the side when
they heard the loud hooting.

"A car!" said one. "Does it belong to you,
little fellow? And is that a dog swimming to
it?"

"Yes, oh yes!" said
Noddy. "That's the
Bumpy-Dog. He was
supposed to be looking
after it. Goodness, he's
getting into it—what-
ever does he think he
can do?"

"Better fling a rope and lasso the car," said
the sailor. "Then we can tow it behind us. What

about the dog? Here, tie a rope to this lump of wood—if he's got any sense he'll jump on it and we can drag him up."

"What the Captain's going to say to all this I *don't* know," said the second sailor. Soon the lump of wood was flung into the water, and Noddy yelled to Bumpy-Dog.

"Get on it, Bumpy! Bumpy, do you hear me? Get out of the car, you'll sink it! We'll pull you up if you get on the piece of wood."

Bumpy decided to be obedient for once, and swam to the wood. He stood on it, holding to the rope with his teeth. The sailors pulled hard, and up came Bumpy and the lump of wood.

He was simply delighted to see Tubby Bear

and Noddy. He rushed all round, shaking himself vigorously and sending hundreds of drops of water everywhere. The Captain heard all the barking and came out of his cabin to see what was going on.

"Wuff!" said Bumpy,

happily, and leapt at him. Then he stood beside
him, shaking himself again and wetting the
Captain from head to foot.

"AVAST THERE, DOG!" roared the Captain,
and Noddy and Tubby almost fell over in fright
at such a loud voice. Bumpy was so scared that
he rushed into the Captain's own cabin and got
under his bunk.

"WHAT'S ALL THIS?" said the Captain, glar-
ing at Tubby and Noddy. "Stowaways? Ha—I'll
show you what we do with stowaways!"

"Sir—this bear has joined on as a deck-hand,"
said a big sailor doll, saluting smartly. "The
other fellow just leapt aboard—and we had to
drag in his car and his dog."

27

"Ho—well, you'll have to sail with us now," said the Captain, looking at Noddy. "What's the matter with your head? Don't nod at me all the time!"

"No, Mr. Captain, sir," said Noddy, his head

nodding even faster in fright. "Oh, do please let me off the ship—and Tubby too. He's run away to sea, sir, and . . ."

"Oh, he has, has he?" said the Captain. "Well, he'll soon wish he could run away back home. Dress him as a sailor, Mr. Mate—and set him to work scrubbing the decks."

"Yes, sir!" said a sailor, saluting. He marched poor Tubby away. The Captain turned to Noddy.

"As for you, you're too small to do anything like that. You can be my cabin-boy—and see you clean it well, and bring me my meals, and take my messages. And STOP NODDING YOUR HEAD AT ME!"

THE SAILOR SALUTED THE CAPTAIN AND THEN
MARCHED POOR TUBBY AWAY

29

"Yessir—I mean, no sir," said Noddy, holding his head still with his hands. "Sir—about my car. I . . ."

"We'll tow it behind us," said the Captain. "It might come in useful when we land on an island somewhere. You can drive me around then. Now—get somebody to put you into the cabin-boy's clothes. AND BE QUICK ABOUT IT!"

"Yessir, yessir, yessir," said Noddy, trying not to nod his head. Good gracious—he was going

30

to sea! Whatever would Big-Ears say if he knew!

"I shall be very very homesick without any of my friends," thought Noddy, feeling that Tubby really couldn't be called a friend now.

"WUFF!" said someone, and Noddy sat down very suddenly on the deck, while Bumpy-Dog licked him in delight.

"Well—at least I've got *you*," said Noddy, giving him a sudden hug. "Stick close to me, Bumpy, please—I suddenly feel VERY lonely."

4. OUT AT SEA

A SAILOR took Noddy down into the ship, and gave him a cabin-boy's uniform. "I want to wear my hat with the bell," said Noddy. "This round cap-thing doesn't fit me. It will fall off every time I nod."

"All right. The Captain will certainly know where you are, every minute of the day, with that bell ringing all the time," said the sailor. "You seem a nice little fellow. Now just you look after the Captain well, see?"

"Yes, I will," said Noddy. "I'm going to be as good a cabin-boy as I can. Where's that little bear gone?"

"Here I am," said Tubby, and came up dressed like a sailor boy. Noddy stared at him.

"You look rather nice," he said. "I like your round hat. It suits you. Your mother and father sent me after you. You shouldn't have run away like that."

"I know," said Tubby. "I feel awfully home-sick already."

"TUBBY! GET UP ON DECK!" yelled a voice. "THERE'S SCRUBBING TO DO!"

Tubby ran off at top speed. Noddy laughed. Tubby was going to work very very hard on board ship!

"Now you go and tidy up the Captain's cabin," said the sailor. "You look a bit queer in long trousers and a sailor blouse. What about the dog? I've a good mind to dress him up in uniform too—make the Captain laugh!"

Bumpy at once ran away in alarm, and hid. Noddy went off to the cabin and tidied it up beautifully. He passed Tubby on the way, scrubbing the deck and groaning.

"Oh my back! Oh my knees! Noddy, let's run away home!"

"*Swim* away, you mean!" said Noddy, crossly. "It's all because of *you* that I'm a cabin-boy, and Bumpy's here and my car's in the water, poor thing, being pulled along at top speed!"

The Captain was very pleased with Noddy's work that day. "You're a smart little fellow!" he said. "My cabin's all spick and span—and you're very quick at taking messages. How do you like life at sea?"

"Well—it's rather fun, sir," said Noddy. "And I do like the sailors, sir. They're always singing."

"I heard *you* singing too," said the Captain. "What song did you sing?"

"Oh, it was one I made up, sir," said Noddy. "It goes like this:

34

OUT AT SEA

I'm off on a trip
In a big, big ship,
Yo-ho for a life at sea!
The waves go splash
And I make a dash
To take the Captain his tea!
The wind goes by,
And the waves are high,
And everything's wet as can be.
I'm kept on the run,
But really it's fun
For Tubby, Bumpy and me!"

"Ha!" said the Captain, smiling. "You sing
that to the sailors tonight—it'll make them laugh!"

So Noddy sang his song that night, and everyone joined in heartily. Noddy nodded his
head in time to the tune, and even Bumpy-Dog
barked when the last line came with his name
in it.

Noddy and Tubby were surprised to find they
had no beds or bunks to sleep in. "Hammocks!"
said Tubby, in alarm. "Hammocks for *beds!*
I shall fall out of mine, I know I shall. I want
to go home to my own nice little bed."

"Well, you shouldn't have run away," said
Noddy, climbing into his hammock. "Oh no,
Bumpy-Dog, I really can't have you in my ham-
mock. *Please* get out!"

But Bumpy wouldn't. He settled himself in
Noddy's hammock, and licked his toes without

stopping. Noddy soon fell asleep, but Tubby
cried for his mother. Oh, why had he run away?
Why had he been so horrid, and silly and un-
kind?

In the night the wind blew hard, and the waves
rose up high. The ship began to roll to and
fro, to and fro, and Bumpy fell out of the hammock. BUMP!

He was very surprised and not at all pleased.
He leapt in again, and Noddy groaned. "Oooh—
don't leap on me like that. And STOP LICKING
MY NOSE! Oh my goodness, that must have
been a big wave, the ship went right on its side.
Now Bumpy's fallen out again! Ha—he's jumped
into the wrong hammock this time—my word,
that sailor soon pushed him out!"

In the morning the waves were still very high.
After Noddy had made sure that his little car

was still being towed safely along behind the ship, he
began to enjoy himself. He sang a little song, and all
the sailors joined in.

> "We're in for a storm,
> We're in for a gale,
> There might be a hurricane,
> Blizzards and hail!
> The sails are a-flap,
> The waves are so high
> That really and truly
> They reach to the sky!
> Whoosh! goes the wind.
> Flap! goes the sail.
> But the ship's going bravely
> Right through the gale!"

But *somebody* wasn't singing. Poor Tubby was

feeling far too ill to
sing. He was dreadfully
seasick, and didn't want
to do any work at all.

"What's the matter
with you, moaning and
groaning?" said a sailor,
giving him a push.
"Give a hand with the
sails, quick!"

38

POOR TUBBY WAS FEELING DREADFULLY SEASICK
AND FAR TOO ILL TO SING

"I want to go home," said Tubby. "I feel sick."

"Well, be sick all you like, but *go and give a hand with the sails!*" said the sailor. "What's the good of running away to sea if you want to go home? Why aren't you like that other fellow with the nodding head? He's cheerful enough. Now go and do what you're told!"

And poor Tubby had to stagger off to help with the flapping sails. Bumpy danced round him, trying to help, and Tubby fell over, and nearly slid down the deck into the sea. Oh DEAR! Why ever did he run away?

5. THE LITTLE MERMAID

AFTER three or four days at sea Tubby felt better—but how hard he had to work! Noddy was really enjoying himself; and as for Bumpy, he had never had such a time in his life.

He fell overboard twice and then decided it was a silly thing to do. The little car still bobbed along, towed behind the ship. Noddy often felt sorry for it. "Never mind!" he called to it. "We're arriving at an island soon—then we'll take you ashore and you shall have a run!"

But before they reached the island something exciting happened. Noddy looked overboard— and there was *someone in his car!* Yes, really! He yelled to one of the sailors.

"Who's that in my car? It looks like a fairy doll from the top of a Christmas tree."

"Well, it isn't—it's a little mermaid!" said the sailor. "My word—doesn't she look sweet in your car?"

"What's a mermaid?" said Noddy.

"Oh—mermaids live under the sea, and have tails instead of legs," said the sailor. "Isn't she having a wonderful time!"

The little mermaid was certainly enjoying herself! She waved to everyone, and pretended she was steering the car.

"The wind's gone right down," said Noddy. "I'm going to ask the Captain if I can dive into the sea and talk to that mermaid. Will the ship go now that there's no wind to blow it along?"

"No," said the sailor. "You ask the Captain what you want to. Maybe we'll see a whole lot of the little tailed creatures coming up if you take them rides in your bobbing car. But mind it doesn't grow a tail itself!"

"Oh, I hope it won't do that!" said Noddy, in alarm. Off he went to the Captain, who laughed loudly.

"Mermaids! Well, well! So they've found your car, have they? Well, be careful *you* don't grow a tail too."

"I wouldn't like a tail," said Noddy. "I need my feet for the car pedals!" And away he went, back to the deck.

Splash! Into the sea he dived, and the little mermaid was so frightened that she disappeared into the sea at once. Bumpy dived in too, but Tubby wouldn't. Noddy swam to his car and got into it. Oh, how lovely to be in it again, even though he couldn't drive it properly!

Soon a good many little heads appeared, bobbing about round the car. Mermaids—and mermen too! "I'll give you rides, if

43

you like, while our ship is becalmed!" called Noddy.

And now look at his car! You can hardly see

it for mermaids and mermen. Noddy thought their tails were lovely. When the wind began to blow a little, and the ship moved slowly through the waves, the little fish-tailed folk cried out in delight, for then the small car moved along too.

"Ahoy there!" called a sailor at last. "You're to come aboard, Noddy. Captain's orders. Wind's getting up and we're moving off. We're calling at Shell Island tomorrow."

Noddy said goodbye to the merfolk. One little mermaid swam deep down into the water and came up again with a pearl necklace. She hung it round Noddy's neck.

"Oh, thank you!" said Noddy. "If EVER I get home again, little Tessie Bear will love this necklace. I do like you mermaids and mermen. I hope you've enjoyed using my car!"

They waved goodbye as he climbed up a rope
to the deck—and away went the lovely ship, her
sails billowing once more, as the wind began to
rise. The little car bobbed up and down behind,
giving little parp-parps now and again, as if it
wanted to tell everyone it was still there.

The pearl necklace was really pretty. Noddy
wrapped it up and put it deep down in the pocket
of his blue shorts, which were packed away in
a drawer. How pleased Tessie would be!

On went the lovely ship—and on and on. Next
day what a shout went up! "LAND AHOY!
LAND AHOY!"

Everyone rushed to the side of the ship. "Shell
Island!" said Noddy. "NOW my little car will
be able to use its wheels again! LAND AHOY,
little car!"

"PARP! PARP!" answered the car, happily.
"PARP PARP!"

6. SHELL ISLAND

EVERYONE was very excited, and the Bumpy-Dog most of all. He tore round the decks, almost knocking over the Captain, and leapt up at Tubby and Noddy in joy. Down they went!

"I said '*Shell* Island', not '*Bone* Island', silly dog," said Noddy, getting up. "Now, if you knock me down again with one of those leaps of yours I won't take you on shore!"

It *was* fun to go ashore. The ship tied up at a little pier, and then everyone went on land, except for two sailors left on guard. Noddy's car was pulled up from the water and soon dried in the hot sun. "It will have to have some petrol," said Noddy. "Come here, Bumpy—let me tie you to the front of the car, and then you can pull it to the nearest garage."

So off went Bumpy-Dog, proudly pulling the

little car. It badly wanted cleaning, and bits of seaweed hung here and there.

Shell Island was lovely. It seemed to be made of beautiful shells, of all colours and shapes and sizes. "I really must take some home to your mother, Tubby," said Noddy.

"*No*," said Tubby at once. "*I'm* going to do that. I've missed her so dreadfully. I'm going to take the nicest shells I can find, so that she can make a border all round our garden beds with them."

"What a good idea!" said Noddy. "I'll take some for Big-Ears too—and yes, I might take some for Mr. Plod as well. I've missed him quite a bit, though not so much as dear old Big-Ears!"

What a wonderful time they had on Shell
Island! When the little car had been cleaned

up, and filled with
petrol, the Captain
stepped in for a ride
round the island. Noddy
was very very proud to
drive him. He thought
the Captain was really
marvellous!

"Sing me one of
your songs," commanded the Captain as they
drove off together, with Bumpy at the back,
licking Noddy's ear every now and again.
So Noddy sang.

"Here we go,
The Captain and I,
Riding on land
That is nice and dry!
The sea is wet,
And terribly salt,
Though I know of course
That it's not its fault.
The waves are enormous,
And when they break

48

NODDY WAS VERY PROUD TO DRIVE THE CAPTAIN
ROUND THE ISLAND

49

You'd be surprised
At the noise they make!
But here on shore
It's steady and still,
No heaving about
To make you ill!
We're all in my car
As happy can be,
The Bumpy-Dog
And Captain—and ME!"

"Very nice," said the Captain. "You might ask the Bumpy-Dog not to breathe *quite* so hard down my neck. Now—let's go and get some shells. I know the best places for those!" It was fun to go hunting for shells with the Captain, because he really did

know where the finest ones were to be found. He and Noddy brought a sack each for them, and they wandered about putting all kinds of lovely shells into them. They left Bumpy in charge of the car because he would keep getting under the Captain's feet.

50

"He's a very *nice* dog," said the Captain. "But I only feel fond of him when he's a long, long way away from me. Tell me, Noddy, who are you getting all these shells for?"

So Noddy told him all about Big-Ears and Tessie Bear and Mr. Plod and the Wobbly-Man. The Captain thought they sounded very very nice. "I'd like to meet them," he said.

"Oh DO!" said Noddy, delighted. "I'm sure Big-Ears will give a party when we get back home. DO come, Captain. It would be a very great honour—especially as I am only your cabin-boy. Oh, I hope Tessie will like these shells—and Big-Ears. I might give Miss Fluffy-Cat some too and Sally Skittle. I simply can't WAIT to get home now, Captain."

"Well, Tubby feels the same," said the Captain. "I don't somehow think he'll run away again, do you?"

It was fun to get back to the ship, and sail off once more—home again this time, for the

Captain had delivered all his sacks of goods at Shell Island, and was now homeward bound. Home! How lovely that sounded!

"Home to my little House-For-One," thought Noddy. "Home to my little bed—and my lovely garden. Home to my own teapot, and my own chair. I'll see Big-Ears . . . I'll see . . . oh everyone. I'll even be glad to see Mr. Plod!"

And now look, they're sailing away again, leaving Shell Island behind them. Noddy put his arm round Bumpy-Dog, and squeezed him hard. Then he lifted up one of Bumpy's ears and whispered into it.

"Home, Bumpy, HOME! What do you think of *that*!"

7. IT'S LOVELY TO BE HOME!

THE lovely ship sailed all the way back to
the little stone jetty in Toyland. HOW excited Noddy and Tubby were!

"Look—we're almost there! Quick, Tubby,
jump off with the others and make the ship fast
with ropes. Oh, we're back again! Oh, I can't
wait to go back to our village and see everyone.
Where's my car? Where's Bumpy? Oh, there
you are!"

The car was safely on the deck now, for the
Captain had. said it had better not be towed
behind the ship any longer—and Noddy had spent
a long time cleaning it. "Parp-parp!" it said,
softly, knowing that it would soon be in its little
garage.

"Noddy! Here is your pay," said the Captain,

putting a bag of money into his hands. "And I've paid Tubby too, though not so much as you. We'll be here for a week, so let me know when we can meet your friends."

"Oh, I will, I will!" said Noddy, who was now dressed in his usual clothes and was feeling very queer without the long trousers he had been used to wearing on board. "Come on, little car. Tubby, where are you? Bumpy, pull the car down off the deck for us."

"Goodbye!" cried the sailors, as Noddy, Tubby and Bumpy set off in the little car. "See you soon!"

"Rather!" shouted back Noddy, feeling very very happy indeed. A bag of money! A sack of shells! A pearl necklace! Goodness, he was rich, and had presents for all his friends!

WHAT an excitement when Noddy drove into the streets he knew so well. Mr. Plod couldn't say a word, he was so surprised. Noddy leapt out of his car and hugged him.

"Mr. Plod! Dear Mr. Plod! I'm back again. Oh, we've had such adventures!"

"But where have you BEEN?" demanded Mr. Plod. "You just disappeared in your car, and nobody heard any more about you. We have all been very sad and frightened, afraid you had gone for ever."

"I went to sea!" said Noddy. "I didn't *mean* to, though. I'll tell you all about it soon. Where's Big-Ears? Oh, Mr. Plod, I'm so happy to be back again."

"And what about that naughty Tubby?" said Mr. Plod, sternly. "Running away like that and making his mother so unhappy!"

"I'm very sorry about that," said Tubby, humbly. "I'm going to be good forever now. Come on, Noddy—let's go home. I DO want to see my mother and father, and give them my shells."

So Noddy drove Bumpy and Tubby home—and oh, how very very pleased and happy Mr. and Mrs. Tubby Bear were to see them! They all cried big

tears of happiness, and hugged one another like—well, just like bears! Noddy went into his own little house, and stared round in delight.

"My little House-For-One! You're nicer than I remembered. How tidy and clean you are—I do wonder who's been scrubbing your floor. Bumpy, what are you barking for?"

"WUFF, WUFF, WUFF!" Bumpy rushed to the

front gate—and there was little Tessie Bear with Big-Ears! They had heard Noddy was back.

How they hugged him, and how his head nodded making his bell jingle loudly! "You're back! We thought you were gone for always!" said Tessie, almost crying with joy. Big-Ears clapped him on the back. "So you've been to sea—well, well, what will you do next! And you've brought back that rascal of a Tubby, I see! Welcome home, Noddy."

"I kept your house clean for you, Noddy," said Tessie, slipping her little paw into his hand. "I knew you'd come back."

"You really are *kind*, Tessie Bear," said Noddy. "I've brought you a present. Look!" And he put his hand into his pocket and brought out a paper parcel. Tessie unwrapped it and gave a squeal of delight.

"OH! A pearl necklace! Oh, Noddy, NODDY! For me! Goodness, I never in my life thought anyone would give me such a lovely necklace. I'll put it on!"

She looked sweet in it, and Noddy was very pleased. Then he gave Big-Ears the sack of beautiful shells. "For your garden and mine," he said. "And some for Mr. Plod too—to put round the edges of the flower-beds."

"Wonderful!" said Big-Ears, astonished. "Thank you, Noddy—you are such a kind little fellow. My word, Mr. Plod and I will enjoy ourselves making our gardens beautiful with these!"

"AND I've got a bag of money!" said Noddy. "And please, Big-Ears, I want to give a party with you—a sort of welcome-home one so that you can meet the Captain *and* all the sailors. They don't sail for a few days, so . . ."

"A party! Yes, of course!" said Big-Ears. "And we'll ask EVERYONE! We'll have an open-air one, with tables down the street. What fun!"

"Wuff," said Bumpy in a small voice. He was feeling rather out of things. Tessie dropped on one knee beside him. "Darling Bumpy! I've missed you so. You shall come to the party too, and I'll buy you a lovely big blue bow."

The Tubby Bears were very happy too, and VERY pleased with little Tubby's beautiful shells. It really was a joyful time. Even Mr. Plod kept saying how nice it was to have Noddy and his car back again, though he wasn't so sure about the Bumpy-Dog!

And now it's the day of the party! What a long long table there is, all the way down the street, full of delicious food. And oh, the flags and the balloons everywhere! See everyone sitting down, listening to the Captain's speech, telling them what a fine cabin-boy Noddy was!

"Hurrah! Hurrah! Hurrah! Three cheers for Noddy! Two cheers for Tubby! One cheer for Bumpy! Hurrah! Hurrah for the Captain, hurrah for everybody!"

What a noise! What an excitement! Then Big-Ears banged on the table for silence.

"Speech, Noddy, speech!" he cried. But Noddy shook his head.

59

"I can't make speeches!" he said. "But I've just thought of a new song. I'll sing it for you!" And this is the song he sang:

> "We're home again, home again,
> Isn't it fun!
> We've been far away,
> But our journey is done.
> We've missed you all badly,
> Especially Big-Ears,
> And dear little Tessie,
> But now it's three cheers.
> We're all home again,
> Just as safe as can be,
> Mad little Bumpy-Dog,
> Tubby and me!"

And now just LISTEN to the clapping.